Princess Poppy

Snowflake

Written by Janey Louise Jones

DOUBLEDAY

Check out Princess Poppy's brilliant website:

www.princesspoppy.com

For my cousins,
Anna, Catherine and Laura Brown,
with all my love

SNOWFLAKE
A DOUBLEDAY BOOK 978 0 385 61487 0

Published in Great Britain by Doubleday,
an imprint of Random House Children's Books
A Random House Group Company

This edition published 2008

1 3 5 7 9 10 8 6 4 2

Text copyright © Janey Louise Jones, 2008
Illustrations copyright © Doubleday Children's Books, 2008
Illustrations by Veronica Vasylenko
Design by Tracey Cunnell

RANDOM HOUSE CHILDREN'S BOOKS
61-63 Uxbridge Road, London W5 5SA

www.princesspoppy.com
www.rbooks.co.uk

Addresses for companies within The Random House Group Limited
can be found at: www.randomhouse.co.uk/offices.htm

THE RANDOM HOUSE GROUP Limited Reg. No. 954009

A CIP catalogue record for this book is available from the British Library.

Printed in China

Snowflake

featuring

Princess Poppy

★

Mum

★

Saffron

★

Honey

★

David

★

Snowflake

★

Poppy was at home, waiting impatiently for Saffron and Honey to collect her so they could go to Wildspice Woods. She couldn't wait to be out in the sparkling snow.

Ding-dong! chimed the doorbell of Honeysuckle Cottage.

"They're here!" said Poppy. "It's time to go."

Mum wrapped a fleecy scarf around Poppy's neck and then pulled her hood up.

"Have fun, girls!" called Mum.

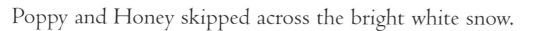

Poppy and Honey skipped across the bright white snow.

Saffron walked ahead holding a big empty basket.

"We're going to collect pine cones, holly berries and
pretty twigs to make decorations for the Winter Ball at the
Hedgerows Hotel tomorrow night," explained Saffron.
"We can put everything in my basket."

As they entered the woods, Honey stopped and looked around.

"Can you hear that noise?" she asked. "I'm sure it's fairy bells."

"Me too," said Poppy.

Saffron thought they were imagining things — although the woods certainly felt magical.

The girls gathered lots of pretty things for their decorations, then, as they reached Christmas Corner, where the fir trees were at their thickest, Saffron suddenly stopped.

"Now I *can* hear something," she said, "but it sounds like a baby crying, not fairy bells." The three girls followed the sound. As they got deeper and deeper into the woods,

the noise got louder and louder and louder . . .

There, curled up underneath a fir tree, lay a shivering baby deer.

"Oh, look!" cried Poppy. "He's not moving – maybe he's hurt."

Poppy and Honey stroked his face with its damp black nose and soft ears while Saffron had a closer look at the deer.

"He's hurt his foot. He needs to see a vet. Let's take him to the surgery – I'm sure David will be able to help," suggested Saffron.

They tipped all the pine cones and berries out of the basket and gently put the little deer inside it, wrapped in their fleecy scarves.

"But what about all the things we've collected?" asked Honey.

"We'll just have to leave them behind," replied Saffron.
"Now come on, it's getting dark already."

Saffron picked up the basket, ready to set off towards the vet's surgery,
but as she looked around she realized that there was more than one path.

"Um, girls, do you remember which path we came on?"

"No!" wailed Poppy. "You *must* know which way it is. I'm scared. I want to go home."

"And I'm getting really hungry," Honey said miserably.

Poppy and Honey sniffled and sobbed while the deer softly whimpered in the basket. Poor Saffron, she was meant to be looking after the little girls and now they were lost in the woods and it was getting dark *and* she had an injured baby animal to think of!

As they were standing there, not knowing what to do or which way to go, the sound of bells began to fill the air and some bright lights shone in the distance.

"Listen," said Honey, "it's the fairy bells again!"

"And look at those beautiful lights," said Poppy.

"I don't think those are fairy bells," said Saffron, "but they will help us get home. Come on, let's go. I know which path it is now — thank goodness!"

They set off across the fields in the twinkly blue twilight.

"It's the supper bell at the Hedgerows Hotel and the lights for the ball tomorrow," explained Saffron, feeling very relieved.

They soon arrived at the vet's surgery, which was in David and Saffron's cottage on Barley Farm.

"Oh, David," said Saffron as she entered their cosy home, "we found an injured deer in the woods and he needs your help."

"Poor little thing, it looks like he's got something in his hoof. I'm sure we can fix this in no time," said David as he knelt down and carefully removed a sharp thorn. Then he gave the deer some milk from a special bottle.

"He's almost as good as new," he said. "Does he have a name?"

"Oh no, we haven't even given him a name yet!" said Poppy.

"How about Freddy?" suggested Honey.

"Or Rudy?" said Saffron.

Just then, Poppy looked out of the window and saw that it had started snowing again – beautiful big sparkly snowflakes.

"I know, let's call him Snowflake!" she said.

"Great idea, Poppy!" smiled Saffron. "Now, I must get you girls home. Aunt Lavender will be wondering where we've got to."

"Oh, *there* you are, girls! I was beginning to get worried about you," said Mum when they arrived home. "And who is this?"

They told her all about their day in the woods.

"Mum, *please* can Snowflake stay with us, just until he's better?" begged Poppy.

"Only until morning," she replied, "because *his* mum will be worried about *him*."

The next morning Honey, Poppy and Mum set off for Wildspice Woods to take Snowflake home.

"Can you hear that? It sounds like something in the woods and I think it's coming from over there," said Honey as she pushed through some trees.

Snowflake's mum was waiting for him at the edge of a clearing. Snowflake ran towards her, then stopped, looked round, nodded his head to the girls as if to say thank you, and swiftly disappeared deep into Wildspice Woods.

Honey was sure she heard the fairy bells again and Poppy thought she saw a bright light flashing past them – but neither of them said a word.

"Oh, look!" said Poppy suddenly, pointing to where they had left all the pine cones, berries and twigs the day before. "Tiaras!"

The girls rushed over and picked up the beautiful berry tiaras, all sparkly with snowflakes and frost.

"The Snow Fairy must have been!" said Mum. "You really are special fairy princesses because she only visits kind and thoughtful people. I *am* proud of you! Now, let's go home before *we* get lost!"

When they got back to Honeypot Hill, Poppy and Honey dressed up as snow fairy princesses for the Winter Ball that night. And when they were ready, they danced to the end of Poppy's garden in the twinkly blue light before they left for the ball!